Millions of years ago, prehistoric trucks ruled

the earth! They were called DINOTRUX.

Millions of years later, their rusty

remains were found and put

into a great museum.

But the DINOTRUX

were growing

CRANKY...

Little, Brown and Company

Hachette Book Group
237 Park Avenue, New York, NY 10017
Visit our website at www.lb-kids.com

Little, Brown and Company is a division of Hachette Book Group, Inc.
The Little, Brown name and logo are trademarks of Hachette Book Group, Inc.
The publisher is not responsible for websites (or their content)
that are not owned by the publisher.

First Edition: May 2012

ISBN 978-0-316-13288-6

10 9 8 7 6 5 4 3 2 1

SC

Printed in the U.S.A

The artwork in this book was created with the
help of 30W synthetic motor oil, 4-bolt mains, and a competition clutch.
The text was set in Ritafurey, and the display type is BigNoodleTitling.

Many thanks to Miranda Stewart
for suggesting the name *Velocitractor*.

IMMATURE
MALE

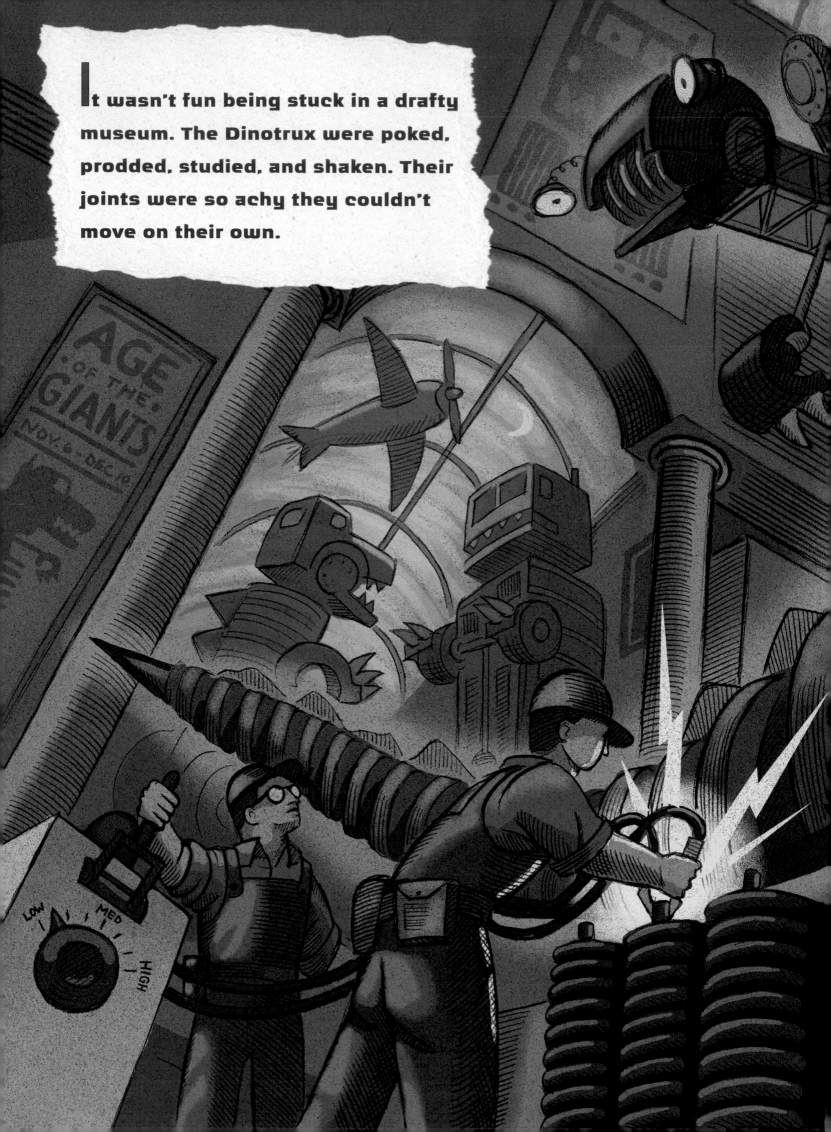

It wasn't fun being stuck in a drafty museum. The Dinotrux were poked, prodded, studied, and shaken. Their joints were so achy they couldn't move on their own.

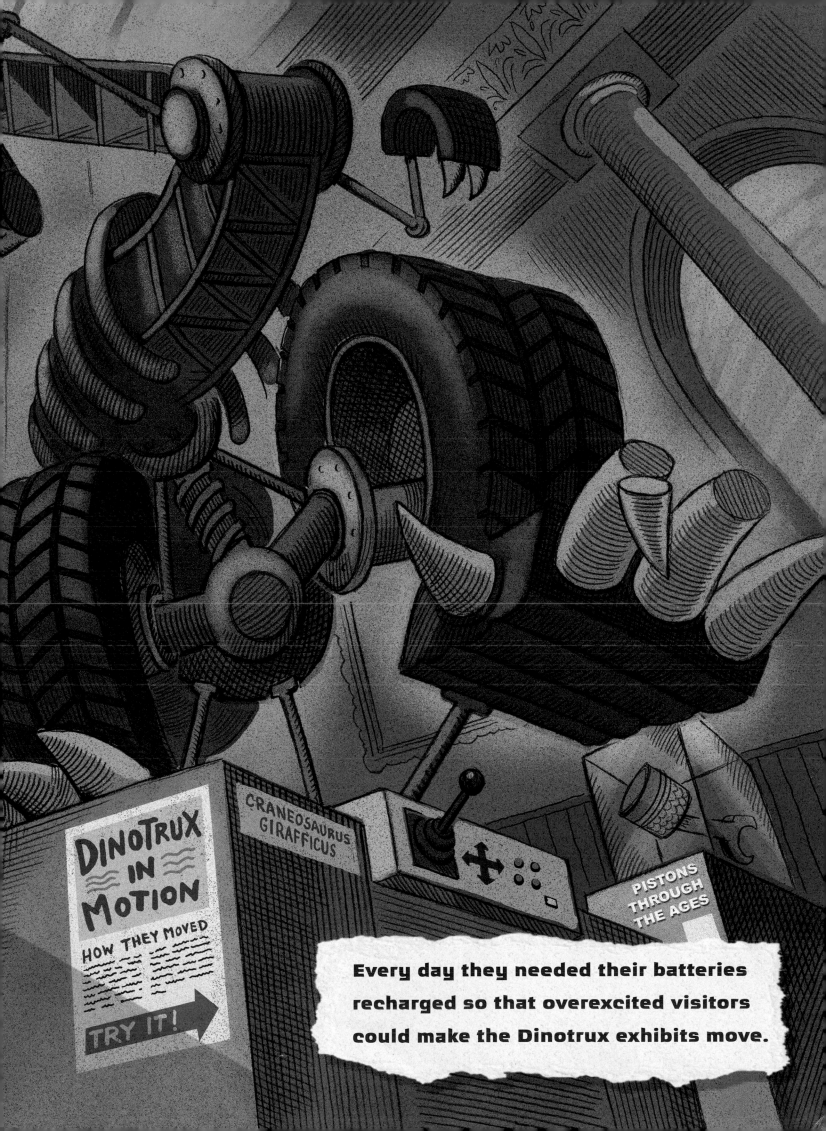

DINOTRUX IN MOTION

HOW THEY MOVED

TRY IT!

CRANEOSAURUS GIRAFFICUS

PISTONS THROUGH THE AGES

Every day they needed their batteries recharged so that overexcited visitors could make the Dinotrux exhibits move.

That night, TYRANNOSAURUS TRUX found sticky gum all over his claws and finally lost his temper. With a roar, he flicked the battery charger to HIGH and crashed through the museum wall. The rest of the supercharged Dinotrux rumbled right behind him.

GARBAGEADON hadn't eaten in a million years. Boy, was he hungry!

Dastardly **DUMPLODUCUS** collected houses.

The **VELOCITRACTORS** did some landscaping on Main Street.

CEMENTOSAURUS left a present in the town square.

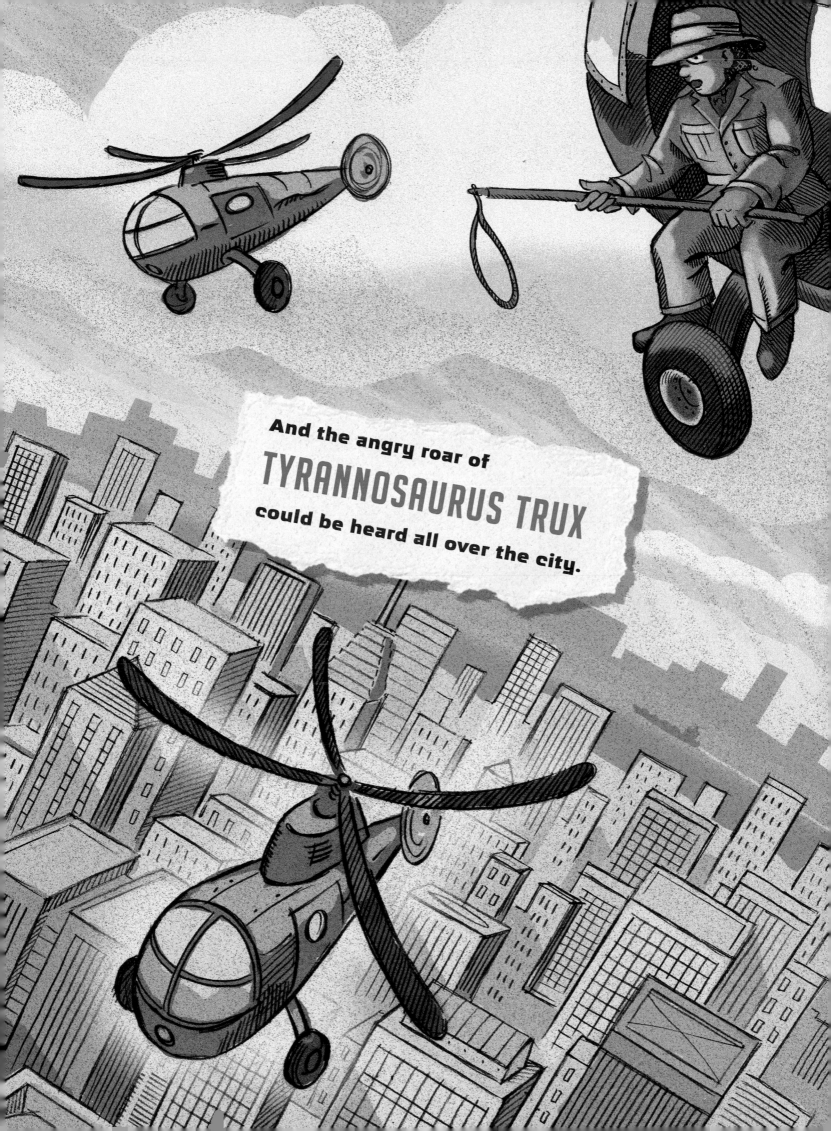

And the angry roar of **TYRANNOSAURUS TRUX** could be heard all over the city.

After a long day of tantrums, the overheated Dinotrux squeaked and sighed and groaned to a halt. The city's mayor arrived on the scene. **"ATTENTION, DINOTRUX!"** he shouted to the tired machines.

"This is not how modern trucks behave. You must go to school and learn new ways," he declared.

MINERDON tried to escape.

GARBAGEADON had a snack.

And **TYRANNOSAURUS TRUX** was especially naughty!

But soon the Dinotrux learned to help.
The children taught them to read.

And together they
discovered some books
they just couldn't put down.

Then one day, the Dinotrux didn't come back from recess. Neither did the children. The anxious teachers found a giant hole in the fence.

A great search led them to the woods outside of town, where they heard a terrible commotion.

They were afraid to look! But when they peeked through the trees, they couldn't believe what they saw. . . .

...AND MAKING FRIENDS.